Adapted by Suzanne Francis
Illustrated by the Disney Storybook Art Team

A GOLDEN BOOK • NEW YORK

Copyright © 2014 Disney Enterprises, Inc. All rights reserved. Published in the United States by Golden Books, an imprint of Random House Children's Books, a division of Random House LLC, 1745 Broadway, New York, NY 10019, and in Canada by Random House of Canada Limited, Toronto, Penguin Random House Companies, in conjunction with Disney Enterprises, Inc. Golden Books, A Golden Book, A Big Golden Book, the G colophon, and the distinctive gold spine are registered trademarks of Random House LLC.

randomhouse.com/kids

ISBN 978-0-7364-3256-6

Printed in the United States of America

10 9 8 7 6 5 4 3 2 1

Even though Dusty was built to dust crops, he was born to race. When he wasn't racing, he was home in Propwash Junction practicing for his next race. And right now, there was nowhere Dusty would rather be—especially with the annual Corn Festival coming up.

Dusty soared alongside his friend and coach, Skipper. "Let's work on that vertical climb," Skipper suggested.

Dusty flew straight up. *Pttt ptttt ptt!* His engine began to make a terrible noise. He felt as if his insides were rattling and swirling. Suddenly, he began spinning out of control.

Skipper radioed Propwash Tower to prepare for an **EMERGENCY LANDING.**

Dusty sighed with relief once he was safely on the ground.

Dusty visited his mechanic, Dottie, who ran some tests.

"I feel great now," he said.

Dusty, Skipper, and Chug, the fuel truck, waited while Dottie looked over the test results.

Finally, Dottie gave Dusty the bad news. "It's your GEARBOX."

She explained that the gearbox couldn't be replaced because nobody made the part anymore. "If you push yourself, it will fail and your engine will go. You'll crash, Dusty."

To make sure that didn't happen, Dottie installed a warning light on Dusty's control panel. "You can still fly . . . ," she said gently.

". . . BUT I CAN'T RACE ANYMORE," Dusty finished. He was heartbroken.

That night, Dusty flew alone. The air was chilly as he soared high into the sky. He watched the needle on his gauge move toward yellow. He went faster. The needle crept toward the **RED LINE**—

Suddenly, the warning light flashed!

Dusty was so busy staring at the gauges on his control panel that he didn't see the suspension tower. He looked up, but it was too late! *CRASH!* Sparks flew as he spiraled toward the ground.

He slammed into the Fill 'n' Fly refueling station. *Crrrreak.* One side of the roof fell onto a gas pump. *KA-BOOM!* The **EXPLOSION** set the building on fire!

Mayday, the fire truck, quickly arrived on the scene. Dottie and Sparky, the tug, turned on the fire hose, but it was full of holes. The hose leaked, and all that came out of the end was a sad little dribble. Looking at the water tower, Mayday had an idea.

"Pull!" Mayday shouted. Skipper, Chug, Dusty, and Mayday all worked together to bring the water tower down.

The structure groaned and then fell. The gushing water **EXTINGUISHED** the flames. The fire was out!

The next morning, Mayday found out that the airport would be closed until he got a second firefighter. Not only did that mean no Corn Festival, it meant no Propwash Junction! Without an airport, the town would shut down.

But where would they find another **FIREFIGHTER**?

At Mayday's hangar, Dusty noticed a picture of a crop-dusting plane on the wall. The plane was a SEAT—a Single-Engine Air Tanker. SEATs dropped water on fires. Dusty felt inspired. "What if *I* became our second firefighter?"

Mayday loved the idea!

The next morning, Dusty took off for Piston Peak National Park. Mayday's old friend **BLADE RANGER** was the chief of the Air Attack Base. He would train and certify Dusty as a firefighter.

Dusty flew high above the **FUSEL LODGE,** a historic resort. The lodge was buzzing with activity for its grand reopening weekend. Cad Spinner, the park superintendent, greeted the guests and soaked up the spotlight. He loved all the attention.

At the air base, the forklifts, tugs, and ATVs were hanging out. Some were performing stunts, some were listening to music, and others were keeping in shape. They were the **COOLEST BUNCH** of firefighters Dusty had ever seen.

"So what is a world-famous racing superstar doing here?" Dipper, a super-scooper, asked.

Dusty explained that he was there for firefighter training. As he was greeted by Windlifter, a helicopter, and Maru, the mechanic, a siren rang out. The team snapped into action.

SMOKEJUMPERS clicked on their parachutes and loaded into Cabbie, a cargo plane. Maru hooked a hose up to Dipper and threw a lever to fill her with water.

Within seconds, the crew took off.
Dusty followed them excitedly.

Dusty gazed down at the fire as it crackled and smoked. *Shoooom!* Suddenly, a powerful helicopter swooped in and dove over the fire, dropping **FIRE RETARDANT.** Dusty knew right away: it was Blade Ranger.

Blade ordered Cabbie to open his ramp. The smokejumpers hooted and hollered as they leapt out, released their parachutes, and floated into a clearing alongside the fire.

On the ground, the smokejumpers used trees to make a barrier. It was amazing to see them in action! But Dusty was flying too low. Dipper didn't see the racer, and accidentally dropped retardant on him.

Blade glared at Dusty for getting in the way. Dusty was embarrassed!

Back at the base, Dusty yelped as Maru blasted him with the fire hose to clean him off. Then Maru installed **PONTOONS** on him. "You're gonna need these," Maru said. "They may be old, but they'll let you scoop water right off the lake."

Dusty thought they were amazing . . . once he figured out how to move with them!

Dusty looked at the photos Maru had put up on his wall. Maru told him they were pictures of planes that had crashed on the job. Dusty gazed at them with **RESPECT**. Firefighters had to be very brave. "They fly in when others are flying out," Maru said. "It takes a special kind of plane."

Dusty began training right away. He flew well around obstacles, but trying to scoop water from the lake was a disaster. The lake's current caused him to wobble and bounce. Instead of scooping the water, he ended up skipping across the surface.

Next, Dusty tried to drop retardant on flaming barrels.
That was a **DISASTER**, too.

Each time Dusty made a pass, Blade yelled at him for
doing something wrong: "Too early. Too high! Too low!"
Dusty wondered if he would ever get it right.

Then Dusty saw smoke and got an idea. He zoomed off and dropped fire retardant right on the target!

Blade came over to see what Dusty had done—and found an unhappy family around a wet campfire. Dusty had put out their fire and extinguished their fun.

Blade was not impressed with Dusty's performance. Dusty felt humiliated!

Frustrated, he went back to his hangar. Luckily, the
gang from Propwash radioed him with GOOD NEWS.
They had found a gearbox for him!

"Are you kidding me?" Dusty asked. His excitement was
hard to contain.

Sparky told him that the part would be shipped soon,
and they would have it in a couple of days.

Cad showed up at the base complaining. "I heard one of your staff soaked my campers with some of that red deodorant stuff."

Dusty apologized, but Cad forgot all about it once he realized Dusty was a celebrity.

He insisted that Dusty attend the GRAND REOPENING PARTY. "There are gonna be a lot of VIPs—Very Important Planes."

The next morning, a lightning storm caused a huge forest fire. Dusty wanted to help, but Blade told him to stay behind—he didn't think Dusty was ready. Then Dipper and Windlifter convinced Blade to let Dusty come along.

The fire was raging out of control. Cabbie dropped the smokejumpers into a clearing.

The wind changed and the fire started to spread. A tree fell, blocking the smokejumpers' path. **THEY WERE STUCK.**

"I see 'em. I've got it!" Dusty called to Blade. Then he flew above the smokejumpers and dropped the retardant, extinguishing the flames!

"Load and return, champ," said Blade.

Dusty felt terrific.

It took almost the whole day to contain the fire. When Dusty and his friends got to the lodge, they looked pretty ragged. They certainly didn't fit in at Cad's **FANCY PARTY**.

A fire truck named Pulaski asked Dusty and Dipper about the fire, but Cad dragged Dusty away as soon as he saw him. He wanted to use Dusty to impress his important guests.

Dusty and Dipper met an RV couple, Winnie and Harvey, who were celebrating their fiftieth wedding anniversary. "And Harvey, bless his heart, is trying to find the spot where we had our first kiss," said Winnie.

By Harvey's description, Dusty recognized the location and gave the couple directions to a canyon near the lodge.

Out on the patio, everyone was talking about different jobs they'd had. "I worked as a taco truck, and then I got into RV tire sales," Harvey said.

"Windlifter was a lumberjack, Cabbie was in the military, and I hauled cargo up in Anchorage," Dipper added.

Dusty started to wonder if **FIREFIGHTING** could be his **SECOND CAREER**.

The next morning, Dusty awoke to **BAD NEWS** from Propwash. The part they had ordered was wrong. "Nobody has your gearbox," said Chug sadly.

Dusty didn't know what to say. He clicked off the radio and stood for a moment in silence.

Then Patch's voice came over the PA. "We've got two wildfires!"

When Blade and Dusty went to check it out, they were shocked at how close the fire was to the lodge. Blade radioed Maru: "They have to evacuate!"

Maru told Cad he had to get
the guests out of the lodge, but
Cad wouldn't listen.

"I've been working on this lodge for five years. I'm not gonna evacuate now just to be safe!" he yelled.

Flames ripped through the forest, but Dusty couldn't focus on the fire. He was thinking about his gearbox and closely watching his gauge.

Even though Blade told him not to, Dusty tried to scoop water from the lake. He hit the surface hard and **BOUNCED** up and down, causing water to spray everywhere and his engine to stall.

Dusty tried over and over to start his engine, needing to get airborne before he was caught by the current and forced down the adjoining river.

Blade was frustrated with the trainee. If Dusty had listened, none of this would have happened. "Keep your pontoons downstream!" he yelled.

The rapids pulled Dusty toward the falls. He couldn't stop! The current was **TOO STRONG**.

At the last moment, his engine started.

"Now redline it!" Blade yelled.

Dusty pushed his engine hard, but when his warning light flashed, he panicked and eased off the power. He hit a rock and went spinning down the falls. *"Ahhh!"*

Suddenly—*CLANK!*—Blade hooked Dusty with **HIS HOIST** just before the little plane crashed on the rocks below.

Blade found an old mineshaft for cover, but Dusty didn't want to go in. Blade began to think that Dusty didn't have what it took to be a firefighter. "Go back to racing and win yourself another trophy—*champ!*"

Finally, Dusty confessed. "My gearbox is busted! I can't go back to racing. That's why I pulled power."

Blade told Dusty that life takes **UNEXPECTED TURNS**. "And if you give up today, think of all the lives you won't save tomorrow."

At the lodge, everyone began to panic. Smoke was on the horizon, and the fire was getting closer. Pulaski organized an **EVACUATION** and began to guide everyone toward an exit. Meanwhile, Cad was only worried about saving the lodge.

When the fire finally passed over the mine, Dusty and Blade went into the smoky forest. They found a clearing and took off.

Seconds later, Blade's engine let out a terrible whine. He **SLAMMED** into the ground! Dusty radioed for help. "Blade is down! I repeat, Blade is down!"

Windlifter carried Blade back to Maru's hangar. When the mechanic had finished fixing Blade, he told Dusty about Blade's past and how Blade had **REINVENTED** himself. This was a second job for Blade, too. He had once been an actor who pretended to save lives. "Now he saves 'em for real."

Blade might have been injured, but the air attack team still had a fire to fight. Traffic was jammed as everyone waited in line, trying to get out of the park. Pulaski sprayed water from his nozzle to keep the flames away. Then a big **GUST OF WIND** blew the flames over the only road into the valley. There was no way out!

The fire raged below. Windlifter, Dipper, and Dusty flew toward the main entrance. They dropped retardant and extinguished the fire. The road was clear! Everyone on the ground **CHEERED** as the traffic began to flow again.

Then word came over the radio: two old RVs were **TRAPPED** in a nearby canyon. Dusty knew right away—it was Winnie and Harvey!

"I can get there the fastest," he told Windlifter, and raced off to help.

Dusty found Winnie and Harvey stranded on a burning bridge. He tried to **SCOOP WATER** from the river, but he couldn't—burning trees and fallen rocks blocked his way.

Harvey and Winnie huddled against each other as the bridge began to crumble. Just then, Blade swooped in. He hooked the couple and hoisted them to keep them from falling.

Dusty had an idea. He zoomed toward the falls. His **WARNING LIGHT** came on, but he refused to slow down. With all his might, he made the vertical climb and scooped water on his way up!

As Dusty zoomed down, he dropped water on the bridge, extinguishing the fire! Blade lowered Winnie and Harvey, and the two quickly rolled to safety as the bridge collapsed behind them.

"Good move, partner," Blade said.

At that moment, Dusty's prop suddenly stopped. He fell from the sky, smashing through some trees. Then he **CRASHED** onto the ground.

Dusty woke up five days later. He was amazed to be alive. Maru could barely wait to tell him the good news: he had built Dusty a gearbox. **DUSTY WAS FIXED!**

"A new gearbox?" Dusty gasped.

"No, it's better than new," said Maru proudly.

Blade gave him another bit of good news. "You've earned that **CERTIFICATION.**"

Dusty fired up his turbine. He beamed as the power surged through him.

Dusty was happy to get back home. Now that Mayday's fire equipment had gotten an update and Dusty was certified as a second firefighter, Propwash Junction was **BACK IN BUSINESS!**

That also meant the Corn Festival could go on. The town was overjoyed! And the best part was that Dusty was able to celebrate with all of his friends, both old and new.